Unicorn Princesses

THE WING SPELL

The Unicorn Princesses series

Sunbeam's Shine

Flash's Dash

Bloom's Ball

Prism's Paint

Breeze's Blast

Moon's Dance

Firefly's Glow

Feather's Flight

The Moonbeams

The Wing Spell

Unicorn Princesses

THE WING SPELL

Emily Bliss

illustrated by Sydney Hanson

BLOOMSBURY
CHILDREN'S BOOKS
NEW YORK LONDON OXFORD NEW DELHI SYDNEY

BLOOMSBURY CHILDREN'S BOOKS
Bloomsbury Publishing Inc., part of Bloomsbury Publishing Plc
1385 Broadway, New York, NY 10018

BLOOMSBURY, BLOOMSBURY CHILDREN'S BOOKS, and the Diana logo
are trademarks of Bloomsbury Publishing Plc

First published in the United States of America in September 2020
by Bloomsbury Children's Books
www.bloomsbury.com

Library of Congress Cataloging-in-Publication Data
Names: Bliss, Emily, author. | Hanson, Sydney, illustrator.
Title: The wing spell / by Emily Bliss ; [illustrated by Sydney Hanson]
Description: New York : Bloomsbury Children's Books, 2020. | Series: Unicorn princesses ; vol 10 |
Summary: Ernest the wizard lizard's spell allows Princess Flash to join Princess Feather and Cressida on a trip to the Wing Realm but when the spell goes wrong, Cressida must find a way to get them home.
Identifiers: LCCN 2020026204 (print) | LCCN 2020026205 (e-book)
ISBN 978-1-5476-0488-3 (paperback) • ISBN 978-1-5476-0489-0 (hardcover)
ISBN 978-1-5476-0490-6 (e-book)
Subjects: CYAC: Unicorns—Fiction. | Princesses—Fiction. | Magic—Fiction. | Flight—Fiction.
Classification: LCC PZ7.1.B633 Win 2020 (print) | LCC PZ7.1.B633 (e-book) | DDC [Fic]—dc23
LC record available at https://lccn.loc.gov/2020026204
LC e-book record available at https://lccn.loc.gov/2020026205

Book design by Jessie Gang and John Candell
Typeset by Westchester Publishing Services
Printed and bound in the U.S.A. by Berryville Graphics Inc., Berryville, Virginia
2 4 6 8 10 9 7 5 3 (paperback)
2 4 6 8 10 9 7 5 3 1 (hardcover)

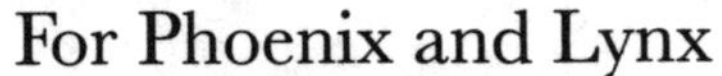

For Phoenix and Lynx

Unicorn Princesses

THE WING SPELL

Chapter One

In the top tower of Spiral Palace, Ernest, a wizard-lizard, lay in bed under a puffy purple comforter. He stretched and blinked as sunlight streamed through his window. He yawned and rubbed his eyes. And then, with his green scaly hands, he reached over to his bedside table and grabbed a book. In red script across the cover, the title read, *Get It Right the First Time: Ten Easy Tips to End Magical Mishaps and Cast Spells with Confidence.*

Ernest flipped the book open to where he'd left a bookmark. He began to read silently from page 38:

TIP FOUR: Read spells while you're casting them, even if you're completely sure you have them memorized!

Many wizard-lizards insist on trying to memorize spells before they cast them. But attempting to memorize a spell instead of reading it is a leading cause of mistakes. We strongly suggest you read directly from your books while you're casting spells, especially if your spells often result in magical mishaps.

"Hmm," Ernest said to himself. "I don't know about that. I suppose it's worth considering. Maybe."

Before he could continue reading, there was a knock on the door. "Come in," he called.

The door creaked open, and in walked a silver unicorn. Around her neck hung a pink ribbon necklace with a diamond gemstone.

"Princess Flash!" Ernest said, smiling.

Flash looked at Ernest, still lying in bed. "Did I wake you?" she asked.

"Not at all," Ernest said. "I was reading."

"What are you reading?" Flash asked.

"Um, nothing really. Just a book about casting spells," Ernest said, shutting the book and shoving it under his pillow. He slid out from under his comforter and stood, revealing purple-and-white-striped pajamas. "Might I help you with something?" he asked, looking hopeful. "You don't happen to need any magical assistance, do you?"

Flash grinned. "It just so happens I do."

Ernest's eyes lit up. "You do?" he asked. "Really? You need help from me?"

Flash smiled. "Yes," she said. "From you, the one and only Ernest."

Ernest hopped from one foot to the other. "What can I do?" he asked. "Whatever it is, I'll do it right away."

"Well," Flash said, "did you know Feather is going on a trip to the Wing Realm today?"

Ernest nodded.

"The rest of us can't go because we can't fly," Flash continued.

Ernest nodded.

"But you know how my magic power is to run so fast lightning bolts crackle

around my horn and hooves?" Flash asked.

Ernest nodded.

"Well," Flash said, "doesn't it seem like if I had wings, I could use my magic to fly just as fast and just as far as Feather?"

"I never thought about that," Ernest said.

"What I'm wondering," Flash said, "is if you might be so kind as to make me a set of wings. That way, I can join Feather on her trip."

Ernest grinned and clapped his hands. "Absolutely! Wing spells are some of the most advanced. And that's why I'm the right wizard-lizard for the job."

"Wing spells are advanced?" Flash asked, frowning. She took a step backward. "Maybe this plan isn't the best idea."

"It's a marvelous idea," Ernest said. "I'm thrilled to help. I'm certainly not one to shy away from a challenge." Ernest spun around and sprinted to his bookshelf. "And I know just the right spell." He jumped up and pulled a thick black book from the top shelf and set it down on his desk.

"I suppose we could give it a try," Flash said. "Can you promise me you'll read the spell carefully before you cast it?"

"Of course," Ernest said. "I always do." He flipped through the book and stopped when he got to page 178. Across the top, it read, "The 12-Hour Pega-corn: Conjuring Temporary Pegasus Wings for Speedy Unicorns [Most Advanced]."

"Here it is," Ernest said. "These wings will last until this evening. They'll work when you use your magic to run fast."

"Perfect," Flash said.

"I've always wanted to cast this spell," Ernest said. "Give me a moment to memorize it."

"Um, just an idea," Flash said. "Is there any chance you might be willing to read it while you cast it instead of memorizing it?"

"No, no, no," Ernest said. "Real wizard-lizards memorize their spells. And I am a real wizard-lizard."

"Of course you are," Flash said, rolling her eyes and smiling.

Ernest studied the spell, silently mouthing the words. Then, he looked up at Flash and cleared his throat. He lifted his wand over the unicorn's head. And, without looking down at the book, he chanted, "Wingedy Springedy Sprungedy Sprore! Make Princess Dash a Friendly Wild Boar!"

Flash and Ernest waited. No wings appeared on Flash's back. The unicorn and the wizard-lizard nervously looked out the window for signs Ernest had accidentally cast a spell on another part of the Rainbow Realm. But no lightning tore through the sky, and no thunder rumbled.

"Oh dear," Ernest said. "Let me try again."

Flash glanced down at the open spell book for a moment. "Ernest," she said gently, "I wonder if you might read the spell from the book. Just as a favor to me. It won't make you any less of a real wizard-lizard. And, in case you forgot, my name is Flash. Not Dash."

Ernest blushed. "Oh, right. Of course." He shrugged and smiled. "No problem. I'll read it as a favor to you. I admit that I do occasionally say the wrong words." He pointed his wand toward Flash and, looking down at the open spell book, chanted, "Wingedy Springedy Sprungedly Sprore! Make Princess Flash Ready to Soar!"

Light swirled around Flash. And then two silver-feathered wings appeared on her back. Flash blinked and turned her head to look at them. For a moment, her mouth hung open, but then she grinned. "Oh, Ernest," she said, "these are amazing. Thank you!"

"No problem, Dash. I mean Flash," Ernest said, winking.

Flash laughed. "I need to go show Feather my wings right away. She'll be thrilled that I'll be able to join her." With that, Flash galloped out of the room, calling, "Feather! Guess what? It worked!"

Chapter Two

Cressida Jenkins, wearing pink unicorn pajamas and a pair of fuzzy unicorn slippers, sat on her bed with her legs crossed and her back propped up against her lime green, unicorn-shaped pillow. It was Saturday morning, and on one side of Cressida lay a large teal tote bag with a black unicorn on the front. Crammed inside the bag were twenty-five books—the maximum number children were allowed to borrow from the Pinewood Public Library.

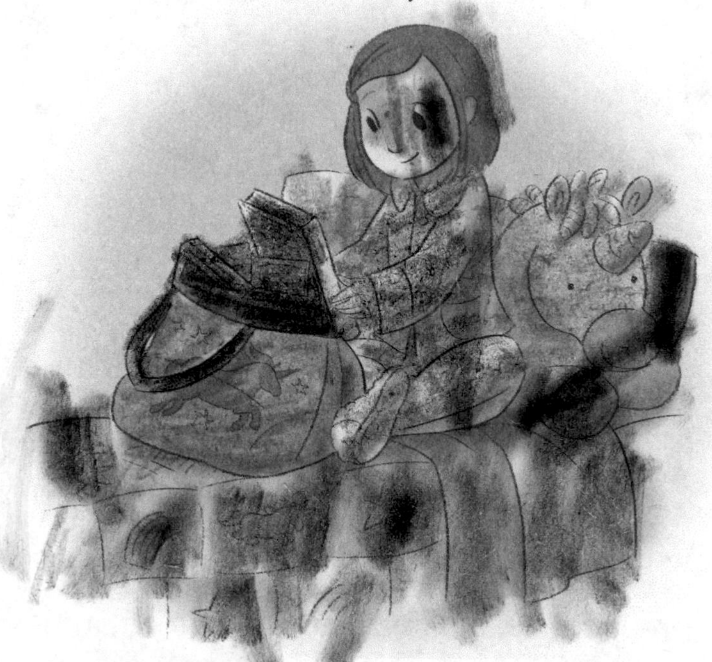

Cressida opened the bag and tried to decide which book to read first. After a few seconds, she pulled out *Wild Animals!*, a hardcover book with pictures of a kangaroo and a porcupine on the cover. She opened the book to the first page to find a photograph of what looked to Cressida like three enormous pigs—except, unlike the pigs Cressida had seen at a farm her family often visited, each pig had two tusks and a body covered in wiry, blackish-brown bristles. Across the top of the page were the words, "Wild Boars." As Cressida read, she learned that boars are wild pigs that live in forests, where they eat nuts, seeds, acorns, roots, and fruit. Cressida thought to herself that she would very much like to see a real wild boar someday. Just as she was about to turn the page, she heard a high, tinkling noise coming from her bedside table drawer.

Cressida grinned with excitement. She closed *Wild Animals!* and put the book down on her unicorn bedspread. Then she slid off her bed, opened her bedside table drawer, and pulled out an old-fashioned key with a pink crystal ball handle. The key had been a gift from the unicorn princesses—eight unicorns, each with unique magic powers, who reigned over a world called the Rainbow Realm. Cressida could visit them any time she wanted by pushing the key into a tiny hole in the base of an oak tree in the woods behind her house. Whenever the unicorns wanted to invite her to the Rainbow Realm for a special occasion, the key made a noise like the sound of someone playing a triangle, and the crystal ball handle glowed bright pink and pulsed.

Cressida leaped across her room and put the key down on top of her bureau. She peeled off her pajamas and put on a pair of yellow leggings with a unicorn print, a blue skirt with pockets, green-and-black-striped socks, and a white T-shirt with a sequined unicorn on the front. She pushed the key into her skirt pocket and slid her feet into her favorite shoes—silver unicorn sneakers with pink lights that blinked every time she walked, ran, or jumped. Cressida skipped out of her room and down the hall to the kitchen, where her mother, wrapped in a maroon bathrobe, read a book.

Her mother smiled and took a long sip from a mug of coffee. “Good morning, sweetheart. You’re up early,” she said.

Cressida grinned. “I’m going for a quick walk in the woods,” she said. Time in the human world froze while Cressida visited the Rainbow Realm. That meant that even if Cressida spent hours with the unicorns, she would only be away from her house for a few minutes.

“Have fun, sweetheart,” her mother said.

Cressida grabbed two chocolate chip granola bars from the pantry and skipped out the back door. She ate the granola bars in five big bites as she walked across her yard to the edge of the woods. She found the trail that led to the magic oak tree, and once she finished chewing, she began to sprint, running so fast she felt as though she were flying. She held out her arms like wings and imagined soaring through the sky.

When Cressida got to the oak tree, she kneeled at the base and fished the old-fashioned key from her skirt pocket. Holding the crystal ball handle, she pushed the key into a tiny hole at the base of the tree. Suddenly, the forest began to spin until it was a swirl of blue sky, green leaves, and brown tree trunks. Then everything went pitch black, and Cressida felt herself falling through the air. She sucked in her breath—this part of traveling to the

Rainbow Realm always scared her a little. But then she landed on something soft. At first, all she could see was a blur of pink, purple, white, and silver. But when the room stopped spinning, she knew exactly where she was: sitting on a purple velvet armchair in the front hall of Spiral Palace, the unicorn princesses' horn-shaped home.

Chapter Three

Pink and purple curtains fluttered in the breeze. Light from the chandeliers shimmered on the marble floors. The scents of lavender and cedar hung in the air. And the unicorn princesses—yellow Sunbeam, silver Flash, green Bloom, purple Prism, blue Breeze, black Moon, orange Firefly, and pink Feather—stood together in a tight circle in the center of the room. Cressida blinked in amazement when she saw two large silver feathery wings on Flash's back. She had already been excited to discover what the unicorns were doing that day, but now she couldn't wait another second to find out. "Hello," she said, standing up and skipping across the floor toward her friends.

All eight unicorns looked toward her, and all eight smiled with delight. "My human girl is back!" Sunbeam called out as she danced in a circle.

Bloom and Prism reared up and whinnied.

Breeze swished her tail.

Moon and Firefly both said, "Welcome!"

And Flash and Feather galloped straight over to Cressida.

"You've come just in time!" Feather said.

"Feather and I are about to go on a trip together," Flash said. "Will you come with us?"

"Please?" Feather asked.

Cressida laughed. "Where are you going?"

"The Wing Realm," Feather said. "All the creatures there have—"

"Let me guess," Cressida interrupted, giggling. "Wings?"

"Exactly," Feather said.

"Precisely," Flash said.

"Our cousins, the pegasus princesses, live there," Feather said. "We've never met them. But they all have wings! A pegasus is a winged horse."

"So we thought we'd pay them a surprise visit today," Flash said.

"Will you come with us?" Flash and Feather asked at the same time.

"Yes," Cressida said, jumping up and down. She couldn't think of anything that sounded more exciting than joining Flash and Feather on an adventure to a different realm to meet a family of royal pegasus sisters.

"Fantastic," Flash said. "What do you think of my wings?"

"I love them," Cressida said. "Will you have them forever?"

Flash shook her head. "Only until this evening, when Ernest's spell will wear off."

Cressida nodded. She glanced over at Sunbeam, Bloom, Prism, Breeze, Moon, and Firefly, expecting at least a few of the other unicorns to look like they felt jealous or excluded. Cressida felt surprised to see they were all smiling and nodding.

"I know what you're thinking," Sunbeam said. "It's true that at first we were really jealous of Flash."

"I was so jealous I didn't want her to go unless I could join them," Prism admitted.

Bloom and Breeze nodded.

"But just now, we were all talking about how we felt," Moon explained.

"We decided that if Flash's wings work well enough that she can go on this trip, we'll ask Ernest to magically make wings for the rest of us," Sunbeam said.

"And then we'll all go on a trip together," Moon said.

"I've even asked the bookworms in the Shimmering Caves to make books for the Glow Library about good places for unicorns to go on vacation," Firefly said.

"Now we're happy for Flash, and we're hoping her wings work," Bloom explained.

"That makes perfect sense," Cressida said, hoping that if the unicorns went on vacation, they would invite her to come along.

"Well," Feather said, looking at Flash and Cressida, "are you ready to go?"

"Definitely," Flash said.

"Absolutely," Cressida said.

Feather kneeled for Cressida to climb onto her back. But just then, a high nasal voice echoed through the palace. "Wait! Don't go yet!"

Cressida heard the clacking of clawed feet racing along a hallway. And then Ernest burst into the front hall wearing his pajamas. "Don't worry," Cressida said. "We're still here."

"I've got just the thing for your trip," Ernest said, pulling his wand from the pocket of his pajama shirt. "I've been so busy practicing this spell I didn't have time to get dressed this morning."

Cressida laughed and braced herself for a magical mishap.

Ernest cleared his throat before he waved his wand and chanted, "Navigably Lavigably Ravigably Glap! Please Make Cressida a Golden Rocket Clap!"

Light swirled around Cressida, and suddenly, two large golden hands appeared a few inches from Cressida's nose. They clapped five times and then, in another swirl of light, transformed into a small rocket ship that shot up to the ceiling and zoomed in figure eights around the chandeliers.

"Oh dear," Ernest said. "I've had rockets shooting all over my bedroom this morning." He took a deep breath, and then he waved his wand as he chanted, "Rockety Sprockety Sprackety Sprace! Send the Rocket to Outer Space! Navigably Lavigably Ravigably Glap! Now Make Cressida a Fold-Up Pocket Map!"

Wind swirled around Cressida's hand. A golden light flashed, and between her thumb and index finger appeared a rectangular piece of paper, folded into quarters.

A satisfied grin spread across Ernest's face. Then, he leaned in toward Cressida's ear and whispered, "It's a map of all the nearby realms. It's possible you'll need it

when you discover . . . well . . . I mean . . . actually . . . never mind. Please take it with you. Just in case."

Cressida smiled and nodded. "Thanks, Ernest," she whispered. She slid the map into her pocket.

"Well," Ernest said, "I'd really better get dressed. Right away. No time like the present." He turned and, as he sprinted away down the hall, he called out, "Have a fantastic trip, and say hello to the pegasus princesses for me."

Cressida, Flash, and Feather looked at each other and laughed. Then, Feather kneeled again, and Cressida climbed onto her back.

"See you all very soon," Flash said as

she and Feather trotted toward the palace door.

Sunbeam called out, "Have an amazing trip!"

"We'll be excited to hear all about it," Bloom said.

"Bon voyage," Prism, Moon, and Firefly said.

"Thank you," Feather said. "We'll tell you all about it this evening. Hopefully this trip will work so well we'll be able to start planning our vacation together tonight!"

Feather and Flash walked out the palace door and along the clear stones that led away from Spiral Palace and into the surrounding forest. Cressida held on tightly to Feather's pink mane, and, for a fleeting

moment, she turned back and looked at the unicorns' pearly, horn-shaped palace, which glittered in the morning sun. She couldn't help but giggle when she looked through the window of the top tower: at least twenty little golden rockets were shooting and spiraling across the room.

Chapter Four

"I'm thrilled you can both join me on this trip," Feather said, as she and Flash turned onto a path that cut through a grove of beech trees. "I love nothing more than having adventures, but sometimes I get lonely."

"Thank you for including me," Cressida said.

"Yes," Flash said. "Thank you."

"It's my pleasure," Feather said. She nodded at the long, straight stretch of trail ahead of them and looked at Flash. "This would be a perfect place for you to take off."

Flash's eyes widened. "Suddenly I feel nervous," she said. She looked at Feather. "Will you go first?"

"Of course," Feather said. The heart-shaped ruby on Feather's necklace shimmered, and pink glittery light poured from her horn. With Cressida on her back, Feather galloped, faster and faster, and then rose into the air. She flew in a circle and hovered five feet off the ground. "I was about to do a somersault, but then I remembered that might not be the best idea while you're on my back," she said to Cressida.

Cressida giggled.

Feather looked down toward Flash. "Now you try," she said with an encouraging smile. "I have a feeling you're going to be a natural."

Flash grinned with nervousness and excitement. The diamond on her necklace shimmered and silver, glittery light poured from her horn. Flash ran faster and faster, until lightning crackled around her horn and hooves. She extended her wings and flapped them, first slowly, and then more quickly. Cressida sucked in her breath, hoping Flash would be able to fly. She exhaled with joy and relief when Flash lifted into the air.

"They work! My wings work!" Flash exclaimed.

"Amazing," Feather said. "I had a feeling they would."

Flash flew upward and did a somersault. She soared in a giant loop. She rolled upside down, so her legs reached toward the sun, and glided backward in the air. She flipped right side up, dived until she nearly touched the ground with her hooves, and shot back up into the air. "These wings are incredible," she called out. "Which way is the Wing Realm? I'm ready to go."

Feather laughed. "I thought you would need to spend at least an hour practicing flying before we left. You *are* a natural!" She pointed her horn upward and in the opposite direction from Spiral Palace. "The Wing Realm is this way. I studied my map before we left, and I've got the route memorized."

Side by side in the air, Flash and Feather bolted upward, climbing higher and higher into the sky. Cressida, with her arms wrapped around Feather's neck, looked down as the trees in the forest grew smaller and smaller. Soon, she could see the entire Rainbow Realm: the sparkling purple ravine that was the Glitter Canyon, the metallic Thunder Peaks jutting upward, the emerald rectangle that was the Enchanted Garden, the rainbow-colored Valley of Light, the spring green Windy Meadows, the pitch-black patch she knew to be the Night Forest, a bright orange dot that was the door to the

Shimmering Caves, and the pink Sky Castle nestled in the clouds.

In another moment, Flash and Feather were so high up that all Cressida could see was a thick blanket of clouds below. The unicorns flew faster and faster—much faster, Cressida thought, than a car, and maybe even faster than an airplane. She smiled at the feeling of the wind riffling through her hair and blowing against her skin. As they soared higher, the sky lightened to an iridescent lavender. Strands of silver mist hung in the air, and small pink and yellow stars twinkled all around them.

"This is incredible," Flash whispered. "Maybe we'll see some of Ernest's rockets up here."

Cressida giggled.

"Keep your eyes peeled for stars arranged in the shape of a wing," Feather said. "That's how we'll know we're above the Wing Realm and it's time to start flying downward."

"I'll be on the lookout," Cressida said. She noticed they were flying past stars arranged in the outline of a giant grinning mermaid.

"That's the sign for the Aqua Realm," Feather explained. "We're right above it." She pointed her horn to the left. "And if you look that way, you can just make out the star-picture above the Reptile Realm."

Cressida squinted as she looked off into the distance. She smiled as she caug

glimpse of a twinkling pink and yellow star-picture of an iguana.

"Is there a star-picture above the Rainbow Realm too?" Flash asked.

"There sure is," Feather said. "The stars are arranged in the shape of a rainbow."

"Prism would love to see that," Cressida said.

Feather nodded. "I can't wait to show it to her when we all go on vacation together."

Just then, Flash pointed her horn straight ahead and exclaimed, "Look! I see it! We're almost there!"

Sure enough, Cressida could barely make out the glittering pink and yellow outline of a wing in the distance.

"Good eye," Feather said. "Let's get

closer, and then we can starting flying downward."

In a burst of energy, Feather and Flash bolted forward, and Cressida squealed with delight and tightened her grip on Feather's mane. When they were right next to the star-picture of the wing, Feather said, "Let's head down to the Wing Realm!"

The two unicorns began to glide downward. The sky changed from lavender to blue, and soon Cressida could no longer see the stars or the strands of mist. They flew through a thick layer of white clouds, and when they emerged, Cressida gasped. Flying creatures filled the sky. Dragons soared by with open wings and smoke puffing from their nostrils. Red phoenixes swooped and dived. Fairies laughed and sang as they jetted around in groups of three and four. Winged dogs, panting and barking, flew in packs. Three brown rabbits with gold wings whizzed by Cressida, sniffing as they passed. Cressida even saw a pair of winged frogs rocketing through the air.

"We're finally here," Feather said.

"I can hardly believe my eyes," Flash said.

"Incredible," Cressida whispered as three winged mermaids flew by, their shell necklaces clicking in the breeze.

Cressida noticed a large silver cat with wings flying straight toward them. When the cat reached them, she did a flip in the air, twitched her tail, blinked her enormous emerald-green eyes, and purred, "Welcome to the Wing Realm. My name is Lucinda." She fluttered her wings, twitched her tail again, and grinned.

"Hello, Lucinda," Cressida said. "I'm Cressida Jenkins. And these are my unicorn friends, Princess Feather and Princess Flash."

"It's wonderful to meet you," Lucinda said, flying alongside Feather. "You won't believe this, but I knew you were coming. I've been so excited to greet you that I couldn't even take my morning nap."

Cressida giggled.

"How did you know we were coming?" Feather asked.

"Well," Lucinda said, "I found a crystal ball in Princess Dash's room this morning, and I was batting it around with my paws. When I got tired and was about to take a nap, I looked in it and saw two flying unicorns and a girl soaring through the sky. And I thought to myself, 'I sure would like to meet them.' I've been flying around for an hour looking for you. I'm excited you're here."

"It's wonderful to meet you," Cressida said.

"So," Lucinda asked, "what brings you to the Wing Realm?"

"We're visiting for the day from the Rainbow Realm," Feather explained.

"We're hoping to meet our cousins, the pegasus princesses," Flash added.

Lucinda's eyes widened and she meowed with delight. "Not only do I know the pegasus princesses, but I live with them. I am their pet cat."

"What perfect luck!" Flash said.

"Will you show us the way to their palace?" Feather asked.

"Absolutely," Lucinda purred. "Come this way."

Feather, Flash, and Cressida flew alongside Lucinda as she wove through groups of fairies, flying rabbits, flying deer, and flying turtles. Below them, Cressida saw a forest that reminded her of the woods surrounding Spiral Palace. "While we're on our way, who wants to play a guessing game?" Lucinda asked, flashing a hopeful grin at Cressida.

"I do!" Cressida blurted out.

"I love guessing games more than just about anything else in the world," Lucinda said. "I like them even as much as catnaps. And that's saying a lot. How about if I guess your favorite magical creature?"

"Okay," Cressida said. She glanced at her unicorn leggings, unicorn sneakers, and unicorn shirt. It was hard to imagine Lucinda would have any trouble guessing the right answer.

"How many guesses can I have?" Lucinda asked.

"How about three?" Cressida suggested.

"Perfect," Lucinda agreed.

Flash and Feather looked at each other. "I know the answer," Flash whispered.

"Me too," Feather whispered back.

"Don't tell me," Lucinda said. "That would ruin all the fun." She carefully studied Cressida's shirt. "My first guess," she said slowly, "is a dragon."

Cressida shook her head.

"Rats!" Lucinda said. "Well, I have two more guesses." She looked at Cressida's leggings and twitched her tail. "How about a fairy?"

Cressida shook her head again.

"Double rats!" Lucinda said, flying lower so she could examine Cressida's sneakers. "Well, the third time must be the charm. I've got it! How about a mermaid?"

"I'm afraid that isn't it," Cressida said.

"Triple rats!" Lucinda said, shaking her head. "I give up. What's the answer?"

"Unicorns," Cressida, Flash, and Feather all said at the same time.

"Really?" Lucinda said, surprised. Then she shrugged. "Oh well. You win some and you lose some. We have time for one more guessing game before we get to the palace. Want to play again?"

"Sure," Cressida said.

"This time, I'm going to guess your middle name," Lucinda said. "I think that should be much easier. Can I have three guesses again?"

"Okay," Cressida said, thinking that guessing her middle name sounded almost impossible. "Would you like a hint?"

"Definitely not," Lucinda said. She looked hard at Cressida and squinted her eyes. "Is it Robertaline?"

Cressida shook her head.

"Rats!" Lucinda said. "How about Alexandralinalona?"

"Nope," Cressida said.

"I'm sure I'll get it this time," Lucinda said, twitching her tail and purring. "How about Oliviariasephine?"

"I'm sorry," Cressida said. "The answer is Erin."

"Well," Lucinda sniffed, "I was close, wasn't I?"

"Definitely," Feather said. "You almost got it."

"One more guess and you would have nailed it," Flash said.

Lucinda smiled. "Thank you," she said.

Cressida's eye caught something glittering and metallic in the distance. "What's that?" she asked.

Lucinda followed Cressida's gaze and grinned. "That's Feather Palace, where the pegasus princesses and I live."

"*Feather* Palace?" Feather said, smiling.

"Maybe on our next trip there will be a Flash Palace," Flash said.

As they flew closer, Cressida saw that the palace looked like two enormous gold pegasus wings. It floated in the air above the treetops, sparkling in the sunshine. All the windows looked like wings, and the palace's front entrance had double, wing-shaped doors.

"Wow," Feather said, her eyes widening.

"I can't wait to see the inside," Flash said.

"Come on in," Lucinda said, and she swooped downward, pushed open the palace doors, and bolted inside.

Flash, Feather, and Cressida exchanged excited smiles. "I can't believe we're finally going to meet our cousins," Flash whispered.

"Me too," Feather whispered back.

And then, Feather, with Cressida on her back, and Flash flew through the double doors and into Feather Palace.

Chapter Five

Cressida thought the front hall of Feather Palace was every bit as beautiful as the front hall of Spiral Palace. Shiny black stone tiles covered the floor. Filmy silver curtains hung over the windows. Chandeliers made of gold feathers lit the room. Cressida counted eight light green and light blue velvet arm chairs. On the walls, painted bright magenta, were portraits of the pegasus princesses: their coats were every color of the rainbow, and they each wore a unique gemstone tiara.

"What an amazing front hall," Feather said, kneeling as Cressida slid off her back.

"It's incredible," Flash agreed.

"Thank you," Lucinda said, looking around and furrowing her brow. "I'm not sure where the pegasus princesses are. They were here when I left this morning." She turned and called out, "Is anyone home?"

Cressida heard the clatter of hooves. And then, a lavender pegasus with gold-feathered wings galloped into the room. On her head, she wore a tiara with purple gemstones arranged in the shapes of arrows pointing in every direction. The pegasus smiled as she studied Cressida, Feather, and Flash. “Welcome to Feather Palace,” she said. “I’m Princess Dash.”

"I'm Princess Feather," Feather said.

"And I'm Princess Flash," Flash said.

"I'm Cressida Jenkins," Cressida said. With a shrug and a smile, she added, "I'm not a princess."

Princess Dash's eyes widened, and her jaw dropped. "Wait a minute," she gasped. "You're not the unicorn princesses I've been hearing about my whole life, are you? The ones who live way out in the Rainbow Realm?"

Feather and Flash nodded. "We sure are," Feather said. "And Cressida is our favorite human girl."

Dash reared up and whinnied. She flapped her wings with excitement, so that for a moment she hovered in the air. "My sisters are all out at a flying competition. I decided to stay here because I wanted to spend the morning reading. But meeting you is a hundred times better than my book. And that's saying a lot!"

"We're thrilled to finally meet you," Flash said, and Feather nodded enthusiastically.

Just then, Cressida heard a loud yawning noise. She turned around and saw Lucinda rubbing her eyes. "I feel a catnap coming on," she said, yawning four times in a row. "Don't mind me," she added as she wobbled over to a sofa, curled up in a ball on one of the cushions, and began to snore.

Cressida, Flash, Feather, and Dash all

looked at each other. And then they laughed. "Lucinda is a very silly cat," Dash said. "She loves naps and guessing games and getting into things. She spent most of this morning pretending my crystal ball was a cat toy."

Cressida giggled.

"So," Dash said, "would you like to see more of the palace?"

"Absolutely," Feather said.

"We'd love a tour," Flash said.

"Yes," Cressida said, hopping from one foot to the other with excitement.

"Fantastic," Dash said. "I just finished redecorating my bedroom with the help of Stitch," Dash said. "I'm very proud of it. Can I show you?"

"We'd love that," Cressida said. And then she asked, "Who is Stitch?"

"She's one of my sisters. If she weren't at the flying competition, you could meet her," Dash explained. "Her magic power is that she can sew, knit, weave, and crochet almost anything. She made me a new bedspread, new curtains, and a new rug. I can't wait to show you," Dash said. "In fact, I'm so excited I wish we could dash there."

"*Dash* there?" Cressida asked.

"Dashing is my magic power," Dash said. "I can instantly transport myself from one place to another anywhere in the Wing Realm." She smiled. "Come right this way."

Feather, Flash, and Cressida followed

Dash up a gold and black spiral staircase, down a hallway, and up to a closed door decorated with a glittery lavender arrow design. Just when Dash was about to push the door open, she froze. Coming from the room on the other side of the door was a strange snorting and sniffing sound.

Chapter Six

Cressida, Flash, Feather, and Dash all looked at each other.

"What is that noise?" Flash asked.

"I have no idea," Dash said. "I've been downstairs in our library all morning."

The snorting and sniffing grew louder. Then, there was a loud crash that sounded like a piece of furniture had been knocked over.

"Oh no," Dash said. "What could be in there?"

"Should we open the door and see?" Feather asked.

"I don't think so," Flash said. "What if whatever it is runs out into the rest of the palace? Or what if it's something dangerous?"

Even more snorting and sniffing came from Dash's bedroom, followed by what sounded like an animal running in circles. "What if it's a monster?" Dash asked, biting her bottom lip.

Cressida took a deep breath. She had a

feeling whatever was in the bedroom wasn't dangerous or a monster—there was something about the snorting noises that sounded friendly. But she agreed with Flash that they shouldn't just open the bedroom door without knowing what was inside. She looked at Dash. "Could you dash into your room and then dash back out right away if whatever is in there is scary or dangerous?" she asked.

Dash paused, looking uncertain. Finally, she said, "I guess I could. I just feel scared to go alone."

"I completely understand that," Cressida said. "I don't like being alone when I'm scared, either. If I were sitting on your back, could I go with you?"

"I've never tried bringing another creature on my back when I dash, so I don't know if it would work," Dash said slowly. She took a deep breath. Then she nodded. "Let's try it."

Dash kneeled, and Cressida climbed onto her back, right between her wings. The gemstone arrows on Dash's tiara flashed and sparkled. And in the blink of an eye, Cressida and Dash were hovering in the air, just below the ceiling of Dash's bedroom. A glittery plum-colored woven rug covered the floor. Grape-colored velvet drapes hung over the windows. A wooden bed, painted violet, had a white bedspread with a lavender-sequined arrow design. And in the middle of the rug, right next to an overturned bookshelf and a messy pile of spilled books, was a gigantic wild pig. It had dark bristles all over its body and two white tusks. It looked exactly like the picture Cressida had seen in her library book that morning.

"What in the world is that?" Dash whispered.

"I think it's a wild boar," Cressida whispered back.

"Can it fly?" Dash asked nervously.

"I don't think so," Cressida said.

The wild boar looked up. When she saw Cressida and Dash, she grinned from tusk to tusk. She snorted, oinked, and sniffed with excitement. And then she rolled over on her back, with her legs sticking straight up into the air and her tongue hanging out the side of her mouth. Cressida laughed. The wild boar was acting just like a large friendly dog.

"What is she doing?" Dash asked, looking alarmed.

"I think," Cressida said, "she's trying to be friends with us. Why don't you fly to the floor? We can always dash back out into the hallway if she's not so friendly after all."

Dash glided down to the rug. She kneeled, and Cressida slid off her back. The boar smiled even more broadly and made an enthusiastic sniffing noise. Cressida let the boar sniff her hand. And then she rubbed the boar's belly. Immediately, the boar closed her eyes and began to make a happy snorting sound.

After a few seconds, the boar sighed in contentment. She rolled over. And then she began to snort, sniff, and oink as though she were telling a story.

"What is she doing now?" Dash asked, looking confused.

"I think," Cressida said, "she's trying to tell us something. You don't happen to know anyone who speaks the same language as wild boars, do you?"

Cressida was certain Dash would shake her head no. But to Cressida's surprise, Dash's face brightened. "My sister, Princess Rosetta," she said. "We call her Rosie

for short. Her magic power is that she can speak and understand any language."

"Really?" Cressida said. "Is there any chance you could dash to the flying competition and then dash back here with Rosie on your back? I think we could use her help."

"Good idea," Dash said. "I'll be right back." The arrows on Dash's tiara glowed and flickered. And then, she vanished.

The wild boar made a sad noise and looked longingly at the place where Dash had been standing. Cressida scratched the boar's head, right between the ears. "Don't worry," she whispered in a reassuring voice. Then, she walked over to Dash's bedroom door and opened it to find Flash and

Feather standing in the hallway with wide, nervous eyes.

"Where's Dash?" Feather asked.

"And what kind of animal is that?" Flash asked.

Cressida explained everything that had happened. Just as she finished telling Flash and Feather about Princess Rosetta, Dash and a pink pegasus appeared in a heap on the floor of the room, their legs tangled together.

"This is my sister, Princess Rosetta, but you can call her Rosie," Dash said, as she and Rosie slid apart and stood up. "I've told her everything. She can't wait to help."

"You must be Princess Flash and Princess Feather," Rosie said, grinning. "We've been hearing about our cousins in the Rainbow Realm since we were born. Now, finally, I'm getting to meet you. I'm so glad Dash came to get me from the flying competition." Then she looked at Cressida. "And I've never met a human girl. You look sort of like a fairy. But without wings."

Cressida giggled.

Just then, the wild boar began to frantically whimper, oink, snort, and sniff. Rosie pricked up her ears. Her tiara, which had a design that looked like a jumble of letters made of pink gemstones, sparkled. She nodded as she listened to the wild boar. And then, to Cressida's amazement, she began to snort, sniff, and oink back.

Relief and joy came over the wild boar's

face. She began to make excited oinking noises.

Rosie oinked back.

The boar sniffed and snorted.

Rosie sniffed and snorted back.

They went back and forth—snorting, smiling, sniffing, nodding, and oinking—for several minutes. Then, Rosie looked at Cressida, Dash, Feather, and Flash. "Allow me to introduce you to Winifred the wild boar," she said. "She's friendly and kind, and she says she's sorry she knocked over your bookshelf. She desperately wants to go home to the Wild Realm."

"How did she end up here?" Feather asked.

"Winifred said that this morning she

was on her way to dig for mushrooms and roots in her favorite spot when suddenly, even though the sky was completely clear, there was thunder and lightning. Light and wind swirled around her. And then, the next thing she knew, she was in Dash's bedroom," Rosie explained.

"Why would that happen?" Dash asked, furrowing her brow.

In a quiet voice, Flash admitted, "I know what happened. When I asked Ernest—he's the wizard-lizard who lives with us in our palace—to make my wings this morning, he misremembered the words in the spell the first time he tried to cast it. I'm pretty sure he accidentally sent Winifred to

Dash's bedroom." She looked at Winifred and tears formed in her eyes. "Now I feel so guilty for asking Ernest to make my wings."

Cressida wrapped her arms around Flash's neck. "I understand how you feel," she said. "But it's not your fault. And besides, I'm sure we'll come up with a way to get Winifred home."

Feather nodded. "We'll all work together to come up with a plan."

"Definitely," Dash said.

Rosie nodded. "So," she said, "what should we do?"

For several seconds, they were all silent.

"I don't have any ideas," Flash said.

"I don't either," Feather said.

"Me neither," Dash said, frowning.

Rosie bit her lip.

Cressida took a long deep breath. She had thought of creative solutions to problems caused by Ernest's magical mishaps enough times to know that the last things she should do were give up or panic. "Do any of you know where the Wild Realm is?" she asked.

Dash and Rosie shook their heads. "We've never left the Wing Realm," Dash said.

"I'm not sure," Feather said. "I've never been there, though I've always wanted to go."

That's when Cressida remembered the map Ernest had given her. She pulled it from her skirt pocket, unfolded it, and put it down on the floor so they could all see it.

Chapter Seven

Cressida, Flash, Feather, Dash, and Rosie huddled around the map. In the middle of the paper was a black dot, and next to it were the words "Rainbow Realm." In the far right corner was another dot, and next to it were the words, "Wing Realm." Cressida put her finger on the Wing Realm dot. "This is where we are now," she said.

In between the Rainbow Realm and the Wing Realm were two dots labeled "Reptile Realm" and "Aqua Realm." Cressida read the labels next to the other dots on the map, searching for the Wild Realm. There was the Cloud Realm, the Flower Realm, the Glitter Realm, the Snow Realm, the Dinosaur Realm, the Insect Realm, the Beach Realm, the Rain Realm, and the Jungle Realm. Then, she stopped. There it was: a dot halfway between the Wing Realm and the Glitter Realm with the words "Wild Realm" right next to it.

"I found it!" she said, pointing to the dot.

Feather looked at the map and grinned. "I was worried the Wild Realm was so far

away it wouldn't even be on your map. Phew."

Flash's face brightened. "Is there some way we could carry Winifred while we fly? We could drop her off on our way back to the Rainbow Realm."

"Good idea," Cressida said.

For a moment, Flash and Feather looked excited. But then, their faces fell. "I don't think there's any way I could stand, let alone fly, with Winifred on my back," Feather said. "She's just too big."

"Me neither," Flash said.

Cressida half-smiled and looked at Dash and Rosie. "You don't have another sister whose magic power is to fly with heavy creatures, do you?"

Rosie and Dash laughed and shook their heads.

Winifred began to whimper, snort, and sniff.

Rosie nodded sympathetically before she snorted and sniffed back. "She really wants to go home right away," Rosie explained. "I just told her we're doing everything we can to help her, but that we don't have a plan quite yet."

Winifred frowned, looking frightened and discouraged.

Cressida saw Flash's bottom lip quivering and her eyes starting to fill with tears. Cressida put her hand on Flash's shoulder and gave her unicorn friend a gentle, reassuring squeeze. "There has to be a way to get Winifred home," Cressida said. She thought for a moment about all the ways there were to carry things that were heavy. And that's when she remembered exactly how she had carried home her 25 library books. Halfway through the walk back to her house, Cressida had found her bag so heavy that she had had to stop walking and put it down on the sidewalk.

"I'll carry it," her brother, Corey, had said, but when he lifted it up he immediately put it back down. "This weighs about three tons," he added.

The two of them paused, looking at the bag.

"We could each try holding one of the handles," Cressida suggested.

They each slid a light blue handle over a shoulder and began to walk. The bag had still felt heavy to Cressida, but when she shared the weight of it with Corey, she had been able to carry it. And, Cressida thought now, as she stood in Dash's bedroom, the bag would have been even easier to carry if it had had more handles, and if her friends Gillian and Eleanor had been there to help out.

Cressida looked at Dash and Rosie. "You don't just happen to have a bag big enough to carry Winifred, do you?"

"I don't think so," Dash said.

Rosie shook her head.

"Didn't you say you have a sister named Stitch who can magically sew anything? Is there any chance she could make a huge, super-strong bag?"

Dash nodded. "She could do that."

"I'm sure she'd love to help," Rosie said. "Though I don't honestly see how having a boar-sized bag is going to make a difference. It won't make Winifred any smaller or lighter."

Flash smiled. "One thing I've learned about Cressida is she has some of the best creative ideas for solving problems."

"In that case, I'll be right back with Stitch," Dash said. The arrows on her tiara lit up. And then, she vanished.

Thirty seconds later, two pegasus princesses appeared in a pile on the floor. This time it was Dash and a mint-colored pegasus with a tiara with green gemstones arranged in the shapes of scissors, needles, and thread. The green pegasus smiled as she stood up.

"This is our sister Stitch," Rosie said.

"Dash has told me everything," Stitch said. "I'm thrilled to meet my long-lost cousins, and I'm glad to make the acquaintance of a human girl." She leaned in toward Dash and whispered, "You're right that she looks just like a wingless fairy." Cressida tried not to giggle. Then Stitch said, "I can't wait to help. What do you need me to sew?"

"A giant bag that's big enough and strong enough to hold Winifred," Cressida said. "Instead of handles, would it be possible to make it with five ribbons attached to the top?"

Stitch nodded. "With pleasure," she said. "Let me just go get some fabric from my bedroom." She galloped out of Dash's bedroom and reappeared after a few seconds, balancing a pile of thick, rainbow-striped cloth and a roll of matching ribbon on her head. She bowed her head down so the cloth and ribbon landed on the floor. "I chose this cloth and ribbon for two reasons," she said, her eyes twinkling. "The first is that the rainbow stripes remind me of our special visitors from the Rainbow Realm. The second is that they've both been magically charmed to be extra-strong. It's nearly impossible to break or tear them."

"That's perfect," Cressida said, thinking that she wouldn't mind having a pair of leggings made out of exactly that cloth. Her leggings were always getting holes and tears in them when she climbed trees and slid down giant rocks.

The scissors, needles, and thread on Stitch's tiara glowed. Magic gold scissors appeared in the air above the cloth and, in a blur of gold and rainbow stripes, cut the cloth into pieces. Next, a magic gold needle with silver thread appeared and whizzed back and forth between the pieces of fabric at a dizzying speed. To Cressida's amazement, after only a few minutes, there on the floor next to Winifred sat a giant rainbow-striped bag with five long ribbons trailing off the the top.

Cressida looked at Dash, Rosie, Stitch, Flash, and Feather. "If my idea works,

would you all be willing to fly together to the Wild Realm to drop off Winifred?"

"Absolutely," Feather and Flash said.

"For sure," Dash said.

"Definitely," Stitch and Rosie said.

"Super," Cressida said. "Let's go down to the front hall of the palace. Rosie, could you ask Winifred if she'll join us?"

"Of course," Rosie said, and she began to snort, sniff, and oink.

Winifred oinked in three loud squeals and ran toward the door.

"That means 'yes,'" Rosie said, laughing.

Cressida picked up the giant bag, and they all walked out of Dash's bedroom, along the hallway, down the stairs, and back to the front hall. Cressida saw that Lucinda was still fast asleep on one of the couches, making a noise that sounded like a cross between purring and snoring. "Will you tell Lucinda goodbye for us?" Cressida asked.

"Of course," Dash said. "But you'll come back, won't you? I need to finish your tour of Feather Palace." She smiled. "Please know you're invited to the Wing Realm any time."

"And you're invited to the Rainbow Realm any time," Feather said to Rosie, Dash, and Stitch. "What we really need to do is plan a family reunion with all the pegasus princesses and all the unicorn princesses. And Cressida, of course."

"What a great idea," Rosie said, just as Winifred began to make an impatient, whimpering noise.

Cressida patted Winifred's head and put the bag down on the floor. "Could you ask Winifred to get in?" she asked Rosie.

Rosie snorted, sniffed, and oinked at Winifred. The boar, with a giant grin on her face, leaped in and immediately lay down on her side. She closed her eyes, looking very comfortable.

Cressida turned to Dash. "Would you mind opening the front doors?"

"No problem," Dash said. She galloped over to the double doors, pulled them wide open, and galloped back.

"Now we need to see what happens if

you each hold a ribbon in your mouth while you fly," Cressida said. "I'm hoping that if all five of you are working together and sharing Winifred's weight, you'll be able to carry her back to the Wild Realm."

"Let's try it!" Feather said, kneeling as Cressida climbed onto her back. "I remember the way from looking at the map." Then, Feather, Dash, Rosie, and Stitch each grabbed one of the ribbons in her mouth. "Just a moment," Flash said. The diamond on her pink necklace sparkled. Silver, glittery light poured from her horn. And then she galloped across the room, running faster and faster, until lightning crackled around her horn and hooves. She flapped her wings, climbed a few feet into the air, and then swooped down to collect the end of the last ribbon in her mouth.

"On the count of three, try flying upward," Cressida said. She bit her lip, feeling both nervous and hopeful. "One. Two. Three," she counted.

Pink, glittery light poured from Feather's horn as Flash, Feather, Dash, Rosie, and Stitch all flew upward. To Cressida's amazement and relief, Winifred, in her rainbow-striped carrier, lifted right up off the floor. "I know you can't talk because you have a ribbon in your mouth," Cressida said. "But swish your tail if you think you could fly all the way to the Wild Realm carrying Winifred."

Feather, Flash, Dash, Rosie, and Stitch

all swished their tails. And then they flew out the doors of Feather Palace and up into the sky.

They wove through crowds of flying creatures, passed through a thick blanket of clouds, and emerged into the iridescent lavender sky. Cressida smiled at the twinkling yellow and pink stars as she tightened her arms around Feather's neck. As they flew, she saw stars arranged in the shapes of a snowflake, a ladybug, and a stegosaurus. She figured those were the star-pictures marking the Snow Realm, the Insect Realm, and the Dinosaur Realm. After several minutes, off in the distance, Cressida saw stars arranged in the shape of a tree. "I think that's the sign for the Wild

Realm," she said, and the unicorn and pegasus princesses all swished their tails in agreement. When they were right next to the star-picture of the tree, they glided downward, through the clouds and the blue sky, and into a forest.

As soon as their hooves hit the ground—and Winifred's carrier gently landed on the soft, mossy forest floor—Flash, Feather, Dash, Rosie, and Stitch dropped their ribbons.

"Phew!" Feather said.

"I have to admit I was getting a little tired," Flash said.

"Me, too," Dash, Stitch, and Rosie said.

Cressida slid off Feather's back, walked over to Winifred's bag, and peered inside.

The wild boar was fast asleep, snoring with a smile on her face. Rosie made soft snorting and sniffing noises as she gently nudged Winifred with her nose. "I just told her she's finally home," Rosie explained.

Winifred blinked and opened her eyes. She leaped out of the bag, looked all around, and squealed with delight. As she began to run in excited circles, five more wild boars appeared from behind a tree and rushed over to Winifred. When Winifred and her friends saw each other, they snorted, sniffed, oinked, and squealed. "They're all saying how happy and relieved they are to be back together," Rosie whispered. "And now Winifred is telling them the story of what happened to her."

After a few minutes, Winifred grinned at Cressida, Flash, Feather, Dash, Rosie, and Stitch. She snorted and sniffed. Rosie snorted and sniffed back. "She's thanking us for helping her," Rosie explained. "And I said it was our pleasure." Then, Rosie's eyes twinkled. "She's about to run off with her friends. Would you like to learn how to say goodbye in wild boar language?"

"Yes," Cressida, Dash, Flash, Feather, and Stitch said.

"It's easy," Rosie said. "Just do this." She snorted two quick times in a row.

Cressida giggled. She looked at Winifred, and she snorted twice. Winifred squealed with delight and snorted twice back.

Then, Flash, Feather, Dash, Rosie, and Stitch all snorted goodbye to Winifred.

Winifred snorted goodbye, and she and her friends hurried off into the woods.

"I hate to say this," Flash said, looking at Cressida and Feather, "but I think we'd better fly back to the Rainbow Realm now before my wings stop working. They're starting to feel a little funny."

"Good idea," Feather said.

"It's been so wonderful to meet you," Dash said. "I don't want to say goodbye!"

"Neither do I," Stitch said.

Rosie frowned and nodded. "We have to make a plan to see each other again soon."

"Absolutely," Feather said.

"Our sisters will be desperate to meet you and your sisters," Flash said. "We'll definitely have a family reunion."

"We'll start planning for it as soon as we get back to the Wing Realm," Rosie said with a smile.

Dash looked at Cressida, "Thank you for all your creative ideas," she said. "Next time I have a tricky problem to solve, I'm coming to find you in the human world."

"I would love that," Cressida said, as she climbed onto Feather's back.

"Goodbye, cousins!" Feather said.

"Goodbye, cousins!" Dash, Rosie, and Stitch responded.

The ruby on Feather's necklace

sparkled, and pink, glittery light poured from her horn. Feather lifted up into the air with Cressida on her back.

The diamond on Flash's necklace sparkled, and silver, glittery light poured from her horn. She galloped until lightning crackled around her horn and hooves. Then she flapped her wings and soared up into the air.

Feather and Flash climbed higher and higher in the sky. When they began to fly fast, Cressida rested her head against Feather and closed her eyes for a few minutes. She felt happier than she could ever remember feeling. Winifred was home. She had gotten to visit the Wing Realm and the Wild Realm. She had made three new pegasus friends and one new cat friend. And she had spent time with two unicorn friends who were dear to her heart.

Chapter Eight

When Cressida opened her eyes, Feather and Flash were already up in the iridescent lavender sky. And, in the distance, she saw stars arranged in the shape of a giant rainbow. "Wow," Flash said, looking at the rainbow too.

"Home sweet home," Feather said.

When they were right next to the

twinkling rainbow, Feather and Flash glided downward, through the clouds and the blue sky. They landed on the clear stone path that led to Spiral Palace. As soon as Flash's hooves touched the ground, light swirled around her wings, and they vanished.

"That was perfect timing," Feather said.

"It sure was," Flash said.

Feather kneeled, and Cressida slid off her back. Feather, Flash, and Cressida walked together into the front hall of Spiral Palace.

As soon as they entered, Sunbeam, Bloom, Prism, Breeze, Moon, and Firefly rushed over to them. "How was it?" Sunbeam asked.

"Did you meet our cousins?" Prism asked.

"What was the Wing Realm like?" Moon asked.

"We want to hear every single detail," Firefly declared.

"The dragons have cooked a special welcome-home dinner for us to share while you tell us all your stories," Bloom said. "They made every dish with froyananas from the Enchanted Garden."

The unicorns reared up and whinnied with excitement at the prospect of an entire dinner of froyanana dishes. Cressida tried not to gag. She had tried froyananas on one of her visits to the Rainbow Realm and had decided they tasted like the worst possible combination of pickles, marshmallows, tomatoes, and tuna fish.

"Would you like to stay for dinner?" Feather asked.

"Thank you for inviting me," Cressida

said. "But I'd better go back to the human world to eat."

Bloom laughed. "I remember now. Cressida doesn't like froyananas."

"That's right," Flash said. "It's the one thing about you none of us can understand. Well, that and the fact you like those weird things we ate when we visited you in the human world. What were they called?"

Cressida giggled. "Freshly baked chocolate chip cookies," she said.

"That's right," Feather said, making a face. "Those things were even worse than the seaweed juice I drank in the Aqua Realm one time."

The other unicorns grimaced at the memory of eating chocolate chip cookies in Cressida's room. "Those really were terrible," Bloom whispered to Prism.

"Horrible," Prism agreed.

"Anyway," Feather said, laughing, "thank you so much for joining us, Cressida. You were an amazing adventure partner."

"And we definitely couldn't have helped Winifred without you," Flash said.

"Thank you for inviting me," Cressida said. "I had a wonderful time."

Cressida reached into her pocket and pulled out her key. She pushed her palms against it and whispered, "Take me home, please."

The front hall of Spiral Palace began to spin, faster and faster, until all she could see was a blur of white, silver, pink, and purple. Then everything went pitch black, and Cressida felt as though she were flying upward in space. After a few seconds, she found herself sitting in a pile of leaves while the woods seemed to spin around her. As the trees slowed to a stop, Cressida smiled and stood up. When she checked to make sure she still had her magic key, she noticed something soft and large stuffed into her pocket. She pulled it out to discover new leggings made out of the same rainbow-striped material that Stitch had used to make Winifred's carrier. Cressida grinned, imagining all the trees she could climb and giant rocks she could slide down without worrying about ripping holes in

her new leggings. And then she skipped home, her silver unicorn sneakers blinking with each happy step.

Emily Bliss lives just down the street from a forest. From her living room window, she can see a big oak tree with a magic keyhole. Like Cressida Jenkins, she knows that unicorns are real.

Sydney Hanson was raised in Minnesota alongside numerous pets and brothers. In addition to her traditional illustrations, Sydney is an experienced 2D and 3D production artist and has worked for several animation shops, including Nickelodeon and Disney Interactive. In her spare time, she enjoys traveling and spending time outside with her adopted brother, a Labrador retriever named Cash. She lives in Los Angeles.

www.sydwiki.tumblr.com